MW01115094

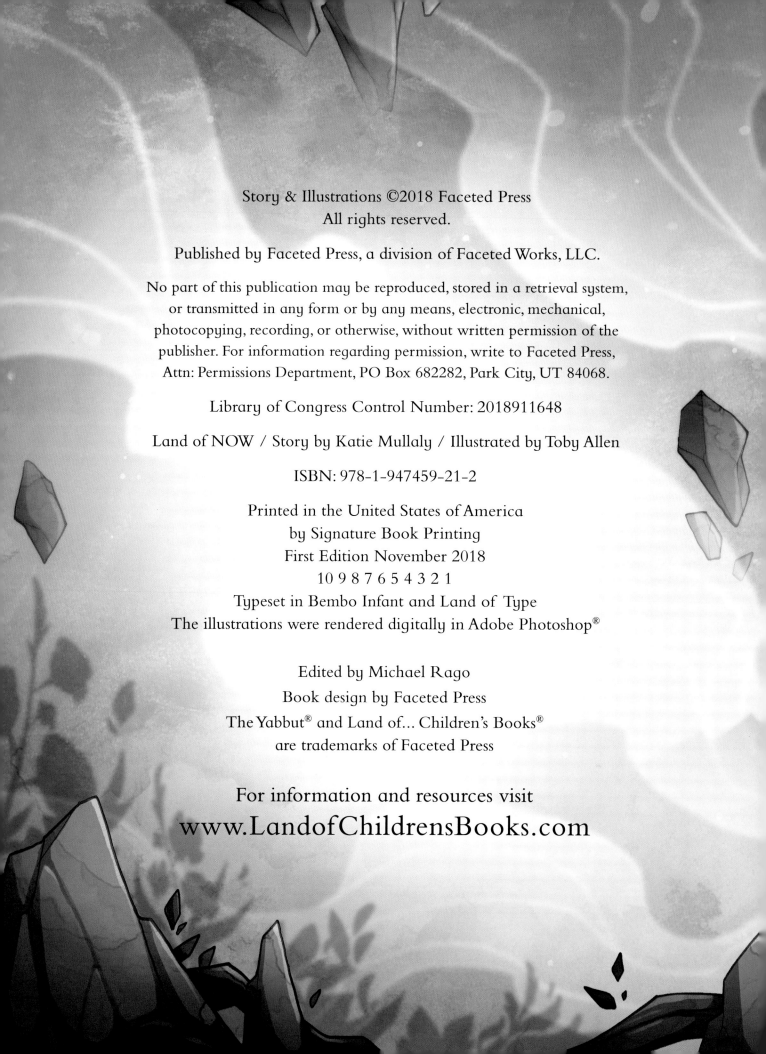

Story & Illustrations ©2018 Faceted Press
All rights reserved.

Published by Faceted Press, a division of Faceted Works, LLC.

No part of this publication may be reproduced, stored in a retrieval system, or transmitted in any form or by any means, electronic, mechanical, photocopying, recording, or otherwise, without written permission of the publisher. For information regarding permission, write to Faceted Press, Attn: Permissions Department, PO Box 682282, Park City, UT 84068.

Library of Congress Control Number: 2018911648

Land of NOW / Story by Katie Mullaly / Illustrated by Toby Allen

ISBN: 978-1-947459-21-2

Printed in the United States of America
by Signature Book Printing
First Edition November 2018
10 9 8 7 6 5 4 3 2 1
Typeset in Bembo Infant and Land of Type
The illustrations were rendered digitally in Adobe Photoshop®

Edited by Michael Rago
Book design by Faceted Press
The Yabbut® and Land of... Children's Books®
are trademarks of Faceted Press

For information and resources visit
www.LandofChildrensBooks.com

Land of Now

Katie Mullaly
&
Toby Allen

There once was a time I was roaming about
Feeling lost and so very befuddled.
I was stuck in a place full of chaos and haze
With my mind all distorted and muddled.

Then I noticed among all the clamor and mess
Someone so peaceful and quiet.
I asked, "How can you sit there so calm and so still,
Don't you see all this ruckus and riot?"

"No I don't, my young friend," said the undisturbed one,
"Because I'm in a place full of **peace**.
I'm in Land of NOW where there's stillness and calm,
But you're trapped in your **thoughts** that don't cease.

"Even though we're both here in the very same place,
Sharing this very same spot,
Your view of the NOW is unruly and wild
Thanks to your unending **thoughts**.

"If you'll sit down right here and let me be your guide,
And take a small moment to pause,
I can show you the reason for all this commotion
And get rid of the actual cause."

I did not want to stop because I was convinced
That I needed to keep moving through
And out past this racket I **didn't** create.
I was certain that's what I should do.

But the guide said, "You can't, 'cuz this place that you're in
Is the NOW and it's always with you.

"There is never a time when you're **not** in the NOW,
It's a place that you will always be.
But because your mind is somewhere SO far away,
It can ruin the NOW that you see.

"So sit down, relax, and we'll clear all this up.
If you listen I can show you how."
Though I didn't believe that this mess came from me,
I sat with my guide in the NOW.

"To remove all the fog, the first thing you must do
Is learn the real source of this tizzy.
What's blocking the NOW comes from all of your thoughts
And your mind always being so busy.

"See, these thoughts are just stories. Most don't have a use.
All they do is just clutter your head.
Once you figure this out, they can pass and move on
And you'll start to find NOW," the guide said.

"Yeah but these thoughts... don't I need all of them?"
I blurted so very confused.
"'Cuz I'm always thinking. My brain's always full.
Don't ALL of my thoughts have a use?"

"No," said the guide, "since the thing about thoughts
Is they're full of this meaningless chatter;
Yammering endlessly, filling your head
With stuff that does not really matter.

"What they actually do is obscure what is real
And turn into a screen that can hide
All that's happening here in this moment we have,
So you miss out on NOW," said the guide.

"To uncover the NOW and get rid of this ruckus
You need to stay quiet and hear
Each of the thoughts that you're constantly having
And let them begin to appear.

"Then you will become the observer who sees
All these thoughts that can mess up your view.
From there they'll become something separate, distinct,
That are outside and other than you.

"You see, you aren't your thoughts, but these things like to linger,
Running amok in your head.
But when you understand that they're NOT who you are,
They can all clear out instead."

I wasn't so sure this would actually work,
But I wanted to give it a try,
And see if my thinking could somehow take shape;
To discover the NOW with my guide.

The first thoughts I saw looming there in the haze
Brought with them worry and fret.
They made me quite nervous of what was to come,
Of a future that wasn't here yet.

I began to stress out over what might occur.
There were so many possible things.
About the next day or the next year to come!
Who knows what the future could bring?!?

"Oh these thoughts," said the guide. "Do they offer a plan
Or actions you can take today?
'Cuz if you do something here and then act in the NOW,
You can keep future worries away.

"But if all of these thoughts only bring with them fear
Of things that you cannot control,
You should just ignore them; they've nothing to give.
Please do not let them take hold.

"Instead, try to bring your mind back to this moment
By taking a big deep breath in.
And this trick will help you return to the NOW
Where these future worries can't win."

So I looked at them all, and I took what was useful:
Actions that could be applied.
Then I let all these future thoughts flutter away,
And came back to the NOW with my guide.

The next thoughts that appeared were of things from my past,
Like errors that still caused regret.
And ways I was treated that still made me mad.
All these times I could just not forget.

"Yes, your sorrow is from what has happened before
But you cannot go back there to mend
Because what has occurred is now done," said the guide.
"The past cannot change, my young friend.

"But what you can do is begin to let go
Of this time that is over and gone.
Only then can you truly be here in the NOW
When the past has released and moved on."

"Well yeah but, I'm sorry for how I behaved,
And still hurt from how they made me feel.
I cannot just let these things go," I continued,
"Because they're still painful and real."

"You're only affected by thoughts from the past,
'Cuz your thinking helps keep them alive.
If you listen and use my advice," the guide said,
"These thoughts can no longer survive.

"You must first forgive YOU for the way you behaved
To set yourself free from your shame.
Then release the bad feelings about all the others
So you can let go of the blame.

"But if these past events offer something to learn,
And apply to the NOW, you will find
That when you forgive, then move on and let go,
You will do things much better next time."

I let the past go, but held on to its lessons
So I could forgive and allow
These old thoughts to leave, since they didn't belong
With me and my guide in the NOW.

The last of these thoughts that were blocking the NOW
Were insisting that things should all shift.
They wanted it their way; to change what was fact,
And did not like WHAT IS and were miffed.

"This pair," warned the guide, "won't **accept** how things are,
So they will not ever approve.
These thoughts will **resist** when you try to let go.
It is hard to convince them to move."

"**Yeah but**, I wish that I was in charge.
I don't like **WHAT IS!**" I then cried.
"But you have no say in what happens out there,
Only how you **react**," said the guide.

"Instead of just longing for things to be **different**,
Why don't you try to embrace
All that **actually IS**, and allow what is **real**,
To enjoy what you **have** in this space?

"And when you decide to be **grateful** instead
For what really **IS** in this Land,
ALL that you have will begin to shine through,
And the beauty of **NOW** will expand."

So I looked all around and I chose to be **thankful**
And then I began to decide
To let go of control and **accept** all that **IS**,
And appreciate **NOW** with my guide.

Then all of the chaos and fog disappeared
Thanks to my thoughts moving past.
I started to see what was truly around.
I was in Land of NOW, here at last!

"Wow," I exclaimed, "how'd I miss all this wonder?
Why couldn't I see it before?
This place is amazing! I feel so at peace!
Oh please tell me, please tell me there's more!"

"What you see," said the guide, "it has always been here,
But the splendor of NOW wouldn't show
Until you had become very present and still,
And had let all the useless thoughts go.

"So now that they're gone, you can start to enjoy
This spot right here under our tree.
And live in the moment, this beautiful place,
In Land of NOW here with me."

"Yeah but, what can I do when the chaos comes back
And all of the thinking returns?
I want to stay here in the NOW," I proclaimed.
"Is there something that I can still learn?"

"Yes," said the guide, "you must learn to detect
When your thinking has taken command.
If you feel worried, or anxious, or sad,
It can mean you are not in this Land.

"Once you're aware that these thoughts have come back,
Just remember the skills you have gained;
How to clear up your mind and be here in the NOW,
So that none of these thoughts can remain.

"Just shift your attention and wiggle your toes,
Then feel the cool breeze on your face.
Or focus on sounds that you hear all around.
It will help you **stay here** in this place."

So now when my mind gets all flustered and full
And the mayhem wells up from inside,
I'll **pause** for a moment and take a **deep breath**
To stay in the NOW with my guide.

This Land of NOW is here for you too,
It's something we all can possess.
When you learn to let go of the thoughts you don't need,
You'll be free of the chaos and stress.

You see, my dear friend, you are always in NOW
So please do not waste one more minute
Being stuck in your thoughts, missing out on what's here.
The NOW's all there is so be in it!

The End

Discover more about this fantastic land at
www.LandofChildrensBooks.com/Land-of-NOW

Fretters
of the
Future

the Kid's

Map
- of -
NOW